Ridgewriters

Anthology

2012

Ridgewriters

Anthology

2012

A Collection of Poetry and Prose

NEW ALEXANDRIA PRESS
LIVONIA

Published by New Alexandria Press
PO Box 530516
Livonia, Michigan 48153
www.newalexandriapress.com

ISBN-10: 1-60915-013-9
ISBN-13: 978-1-60915-013-6

This book contains works of fiction. The names, characters, and events portrayed in this book are entirely fictitious, and are the product of the authors' imagination. Any resemblance to any actual person–living, dead, or otherwise—is entirely coincidental.

"Snowbound with Blowgun" © 1998 by Ginny Grush; "Night of the Living Pumpkins," "Fast Times and Euclid Beach © 2007 by Ginny Grush; "Bad News Bears" and "Intoxication" © 2009 by Ginny Grush "Diamond in the Roughage © 2011 by Ginny Grush

"Aliens in our Midst" © 2009 by Jeffrey Caminsky; "Every Other Weekend" and "Hunting Season" © 2011 by Jeffrey Caminsky

"Love More" and "Elysian Fields" © 2006 by Lori Goff; " Sunshine Angel" and "Satin Sheets"and "Wild Rose Memories" © 2009 by Lori Goff

"Three Birthdays" © 2008 by Wallace Caminsky

Except from The Translator © 2006 by Kathy Beaman; synopsis of Busua Pleasure Beach © 2001 by Kathy Beaman

"Second Violin Mother" © 2004 by Betty Ruddy

Cover design and illustrations © 2012 by Jeffrey Caminsky

Quantity discounts are available on bulk purchases of this book. Special books or book excerpts can also be made available to fit specific needs. For information, please contact *sales@newalexandriapress.com* or send written inquiries to New Alexandria Press, PO Box 530516, Livonia, Michigan 48153.

Printed in the United States of America
10 9 8 7 6 5 4 3 2

CONTENTS

Ridgewriters
Anthology
2012

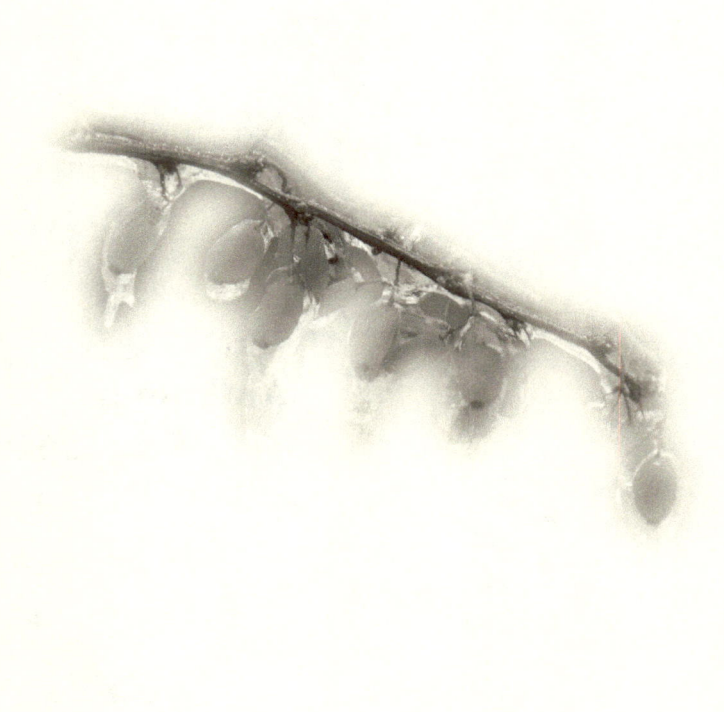

GINNY GRUSH

GINNY GRUSH, a Spanish teacher living in Farmington Hills, Michigan, was once a Peace Corps volunteer in Bolivia. She's married, and has two grown children and one grandchild. She writes personal essays, poetry and short stories. She's been published in *The MacGuffin*, the *Detroit Free Press*, the *Farmington Observer*, and *Peninsula Poets*.

Acknowledgments
"Snowbound with Blowgun" was first published in *The MacGuffin*, Volume XV Number II

"Night of the Living Pumpkins" was first published in Poetry Society of Michigan's *Penninsula Poets*, Fall 2007

"Fast Times at Euclid Beach" was first published in *Penninsula Poets*, Fall 2007, winning 2nd place in free verse of PSM 2007 contest

"Bad News Bear" was awarded 3rd place in the 2009 Albert Anthony Creative Writing contest.

"Intoxication" and "Diamond in the Roughage" first appeared in *Peninsula Poets*.

Snowbound with Blowgun

MY HUSBAND'S COUSIN, Walt, is a man of precision, spit-and-polish. A navy engineer and father of four, Walt can charm the shine right off "the Brass" as well as finish assignments on time and under budget. Walt is also a man of diabolic and perverse nature, a prankster with sadistic tendencies which come from his years of bossing and tormenting three younger sisters.

Walt makes it a practice to initiate young couples to the joys of parenthood by sending their offspring gratingly noisy toys: tinny metal drums; clangy bells; clickety, ratchety pull toys; whiny dolls.

So, when I accepted the package delivered to our house, late one blizzardy February afternoon, it was with a slight bit of trepidation. The return address was that of Walt and his family at their new site in the Philippines. In their Christmas card they had explained that, due to settling in, our kids' present would arrive late. This must be it.

My husband had beaten the storm home on this Friday, and the kids were already lamenting the fact that if we were snowed in, they wouldn't miss any school. We gathered around the kitchen table and my husband slit open the box. Son and daughter started pulling out wadded up newspaper until a long, shiny tube of bamboo appeared. It was highly lacquered and circled at top and bottom with multi-colored feathers.

"Kind of big for a flute," I offered.

"Hey, here's something else."

"Let me see."

The kids were talking at once as they dumped the contents of a brown paper bag onto the place mats. A dozen, lethal-looking, three-and-half-inch metal spikes, protruding from inch-long, ridged wooden bases lay below us.

"Darts," said my husband, an almost reverential tone in his voice. "And a real *Philippines blowgun.*"

"A *blowgun,*" the kids repeated, their eyes now widened to near-saucer size.

Before I could think or act to grab the ammunition, I saw my husband, a usually rational statistician-type, snatch, load, puff out his cheeks, and then *phfffft— thwaaack,* shoot a dart right across the kitchen and into a slat of my expensive woven wood window shade.

"*Nooooooo,*" I screamed, gathering the rest of the darts, running to the window and pulling the just-shot dart out of the slat, which now had a neat, round, little hole in it.

I started reciting the litany of all the horrible things I envisioned happening if this blowgun were ever allowed to be used again: eyes shot out, pets killed, windows broken, gangrenous wounds inflicted, my children's psyches warped, darts inhaled. I ended with the threat of me divorcing my husband and his homicidal relatives, and added a prayer that somewhere on an outer island of the Philippines, a stone-age medicine man was right now putting a curse on Walt.

It was to no avail. My husband, daughter and son banded against me and worked all evening on a plan for a safe shooting range in the basement. Though I was never convinced that "safe shooting range" was not an oxymoron, I finally admitted that the setup my mutinous crew came up with just might work.

Only one friend and no pets were to be allowed down in the basement during shooting. Most important: *Dad had to be there at all times*. The target was the cardboard side of an old packing crate with a yellow poster paint bull's eye hastily dabbed on it. It leaned against the north basement wall.

The shooter and everyone else had to stand behind a chalk line twelve feet back.

And, when all the darts were shot, the shooter had to put the gun down and retrieve them before shooting could start again.

Throughout that long, snowy Saturday, I heard the *phfffts* and *thwaaacks* of darts being shot into cardboard. These were followed by squeals of satisfaction or moans of disappointment and both were followed by the jerks and cringes of my nerves. When I went down to check, at intervals, I noted a bull's-eye pock-marked with strikes, but also darts with points getting duller and duller.

By Sunday I was hearing *clicks* and *splats*. The dulling of the dart points had caused the shooters to get creative again. The old toy boxes had been raided, so that the target now included the armless and legless Planet of the Apes figures as well as Ballerina Barbie and Nehru-jacketed Ken. These were duct taped to the cardboard, Barbie with her ponytail straight up. The dull darts made neat little clicks as they bounced off the hard plastic figures and onto the cement floor. Also spit wads were being used as alternate ammo. These made interesting, if disgusting, white blob splatters all over the targets. I wondered if I could plead cabin fever as the reason that my family had turned psycho.

Monday, with the snowstorm over and everyone back to work and school, I went down to put the darts and gun away forever. Barbie caught my eye. Only one dart had anywhere near a decent tip left.

"*Thwaaack*." Just a little to the left. I retrieved and reloaded.

"*Click*." A bounce to the floor.

"*Phffft*." I parted that platinum mane and felt equal parts primordial thrill and guilt.

*   *   *

WALT'S A GRANDFATHER now, and knowing that he'll be unwrapping Christmas presents with his grandson this year, I'm already thinking of gifts. How about a green slime shooter or a termite farm? Hmmm. I do know where there's a used blowgun. Maybe I'll just sharpen some points.

Detroit – 2009

Hard Times,
do not harden my heart.
Today, I am not sorry for
The Man With No Feet.
Today, I feel only
the cold of the pavement,
the cut of the stones.
Today, I need shoes.
And he has none to give.

Bad News Bear

We're discontent,
malcontent,
unemployed
and under stress.
Wall Street sends
no remedy
and Washington
just B.S.

Night of the Living Pumpkins

They spliced and sliced genetically—
those bio-engineers.
And the pumpkin DNA they made
was remarkable—if a bit queer.

Resistant to virus and bruising
its offspring would weigh one ton.
Thus mammoth jack-o-lanterns
could be carved for Halloween fun.

But the scientists were hasty
or perhaps just a little lax,
for into their DNA birthing dish
fell a speck of genetic trash.

Just a bit of Venus Fly Trap
combined with the fledgling veg
adding aggressive tendencies
and a taste for living flesh.

So when this autumn's bounty
ripens in fields and dells,
an orange, carnivorous crop will wait
the pumpkin harvest from Hell.

Fast Times at Euclid Beach

How good they felt
those heart-grabbing, gut-churning,
head-knocking, butt-thumping,
amusement park rides.
Back when nothing could go too fast.
Our parents on benches, not far away,
praying for a whiff of cool lake breeze.
We kids, all damp and sticky,
headed moth-like for the thrills.
Seduced by speed and daring,
how we could hardly wait
to feel stomachs suspended
as the Cyclone crested the hill,
to be wave-slapped into drenching
at the bottom of the Old Mill Race,
to be plastered to our seat backs
as the Tilt-a-Whirl rose and fell,
to ram each other silly
in the Dodgem's theater of war.
For all those spins, jerks, lurches
and death-defying drops
we could hardly wait.
And how good it felt
back when nothing could go too fast.

Intoxication

May moon rises
crisp, pale and full.
Shines on snow and
white apple blossoms.
Walking my dog
and cursing the chill,
I enter a heady perfume.
Inhaling to lungburst,
then, drunk, craving more,
I linger in
the orchard
to binge.

A Diamond in the Roughage

I shouldn't of et the evidence
that diamond ring I stole.
Now I'm in the clink in trouble
Johnny Law at my toilet bowl.
Yet with push and shout
roughage in roughage out
nuttin' ain't passed yet but time.
Lord, I shouldn't of et that diamond.
Guess thievin's not my line.
And I do repent
know my punishment's
that my ill-gotten gain's now stuck.
And, oh misery, colonoscopy
may be my only luck.
No, I shouldn't of et that piece of ice.
To the straight and narrow I'll bend.
My innards have all been tellin' me
diamonds ain't a gut's best friend.

JEFFREY CAMINSKY

JEFFREY CAMINSKY, a lifelong resident of Planet Earth, lives in Michigan with his wife and family. His books include the *Guardians of Peace*, a four-volume science-fiction adventure series; a book about soccer officiating, *The Referee's Survival Guide*; and *The Sonnets of William Shakespeare*, a guide to Elizabethan poetry. In an alternate reality, he recently retired from a career as a public prosecutor in Detroit.

Acknowledgments
The story "Aliens in our Midst" is an excerpt from the novel *The Star Dancers*, published by New Alexandria Press. "Every Other Weekend" and "Hunting Season" first appeared in *Clever Fiction*.

Aliens in our Midst

"Ys'SLALT—FETCH ME the kettle. Bl'Dryna—I will need the stewing spices. Gal'Kisl, the sauces will need constant monitoring. No, no—Slalt, you fool, not the simmering pot! The kettle—the large, black kettle!"

Like his friends, ls'Shen raced about trying to obey Ra'Henl's instructions, secretly cursing the old foodmaster's reluctance to see one task through to completion before commencing the next.

"Dryna—Kisl—come. Attend me. Ys'Slalt, pay heed. What we need now is the barest hint of jizril seeds in the sauce...."

As the Foodmaster's back was turned, and knowing that he would not be missed for quite a while, ls'Shen stepped lightly into the outer cooking chamber and peered through the curtain. The Banquet Hall was filled to capacity. Dignitaries of all ranks and races graced the Table of Honor. At the lesser tables he could see the courtiers in attendance, and smiled to see the jugglers and clowns and acrobats, their faces streaked with ornamental paint, frolicking on the amusement floor in the middle of the room. From the far end of the banquet hall he could hear the palace musicians, playing a sprightly dance.

But what drew his attention were not the entertainers,

nor eminences that he recognized by name or by face. What captured his eyes were the four creatures seated near the center of the Table of Honor between Lady Glishenda and her brother-in-law, the Expanse Minister himself. Raptly he stared, his eyes widened like a gawkhen's, until a gentle tap on his back caused him to jump nearly to the ceiling.

"Shen—Shen," whispered Jarenda, the foodservant. Ls'Shen's gill slits paled with fright. He had been so absorbed with watching the Terrans that he had failed to sense her approach. "How come you—"

"Jarenda, please," he interrupted, vainly trying to recover his dignity. "Never approach a foodmaster or his apprentice in such a fashion. It is entirely too disruptive. And under other circumstances— "

"You mean," Jarenda smiled, her eyes laughing merrily, "had you not been gaping at the longnoses."

Ls'Shen snorted angrily, only to rediscover that this female found his temper an endless source of amusement. Jarenda was becoming entirely too familiar, he thought, but like all males he found a female's playful teasing too enticing to resist. And so long as they were alone, he took no steps to disrupt the growing warmth of their bond.

"They look different than I had imagined," he said at last, peering through the curtain once more. "Not nearly as furry. And their snouts are not at all what I expected. They are pointed, and their faces wear a comical look about them. Calling them 'longnoses' is something of a misnomer, I think. 'Pointy-snouts' would be more accurate."

"Well," Jarenda whispered, poking her own head through the curtains, "the name 'Strange Ones' is certainly appropriate."

"That I do not doubt, but why do you say so? What have you seen?"

"Look at them," she motioned with her head. "All four of them sweat like wild hogs and yet they insist on wearing clothing. All of them, without exception."

"Yes, I see," said Is'Shen. And sure enough, two of them were clad in garments of blue, and two wore clothing of varying hues. But all four of them were fully clothed, though even from this distance he could see perspiration dripping from them like water from a fountain. Even the Veshnans did not carry matters to such extremes, and of all the races of the Grand Alliance, the Veshnan approach to garments was the most impractical.

"And their eating habits leave much to be desired," Jarenda continued. "See the blueclad Terran male, the one seated next to Glishenda, the Minister's Consort-of-the Day?"

"Yes."

"After looking at his sidebowl for the longest time, he finally asked an interpreter the purpose of the washed sand."

"To aid in digestion," said Is'Shen, answering the obvious.

"Well, upon hearing the answer, the Terran sampled some—using his spoon to carry it to his mouth, of all things."

"Incredible."

"Then he spat it out—all over the table—and started coughing and protruding his tongue from his mouth like a small one with the heaves."

"Amazing," said Ls'Shen, looking at the one Jarenda had mentioned, who seemed to be viewing his broadleaf salad with some degree of suspicion. The Terran jabbed the greens with his cutlery and examined each fresh pepper carefully before stuffing it into his mouth.

"How can you tell the males from the females?" asked the young apprentice. "I mean, if they are fully clothed and all. It must get rather confusing for them."

"Well," agreed Jarenda, "that does pose several problems."

Ls'Shen closed the curtain and sighed. Much about these Strange Ones simply defied explanation.

"They seem to crop their fur differently, but from what I have observed there appears to be but one sure way to tell them apart."

"And what is that, my little friend?"

"Terran females are...well, more rounded than their males," she said, searching for a way to explain the unexplainable. "And they seem to have these—these—bumps— "

"Bumps?"

"Yes—bumps—little mounds—crests really, right in the middle of their chests."

Ls'Shen peered through the curtain once more, straining to get a good look at the Terrans. By chance, one of them turned to the right, just enough to give him a view in profile, and a benevolent Fate decreed that it would be one of the Crested Ones.

"Amazing," he said. For sure enough, there they were, exactly as Jarenda had described. And now that he knew where to look, he saw that the smaller of the blueclads displayed the same prominent features. Less pronounced, perhaps, but unmistakable nonetheless.

"What are they for?"

Jarenda shrugged. "I thought it impolite to ask," she replied.

Soon, the voice of Ra'Henl came bellowing from the kitchen, summoning his apprentices from all corners of his kitchen to assist in circumventing some new disaster. Beaming with a depth of feeling, ls'Shen nodded at Jarenda, who flushed shyly as she returned to her duties.

"Ls'Shen! Shen, come at once! Where are you, Young One?"

"Yes, Grand One, I am coming." With a smiling heart, ls'Shen returned to the kitchen, where he had duties of his own that needed tending.

Every Other Weekend

"WELL, THAT'S JUST great," said Dave, gazing at his shoe.

Or, more precisely, at the dairy by-product passing for ice cream now covering his shoe.

Not that he had anything against ice cream: as a boy, it was probably his favorite dessert. Every Sunday, his grandfather took him to the corner dairy for a treat slathered in as many toppings as he could fit into a bowl, and Dave still smiled fondly at the memory of ordering two full banana splits once, when his parents raised his allowance. And he'd have finished the second one if he hadn't vomited all over Penneman's Store. It took two years before Old Man Penneman let Dave back into the place, and the shopkeeper had viewed the young troublemaker with suspicion ever since.

"I'm so sorry!" exclaimed a pretty young blonde running toward Dave.

"That's all right," Dave lied. "I never liked those shoes anyway."

"I don't know why that place heaps such big scoops onto such small cones," the young mother said, leading her crying young son inside, hoping to assuage his grief with more ice cream.

"I know perfectly well why they do that," muttered Dave, trying to clean his shoe.

From the bench outside the ice cream parlor, Dave had a great view of the parking lot. As usual he'd rather have this rendezvous someplace else: the library, perhaps. Maybe the park. The benches at the park were just as uncomfortable, but the trees and river were prettier to look at than the traffic signs and concrete visible from the strip mall.

Looking up, past the branches of the shedding trees, Dave saw gray clouds gathering overhead. Recently most of his days were gray, even those he got to spend with his son. If the weather reports were right, the whole weekend would see nothing but rain. Not the way he wanted it, but then the weather had ruined his last two visits. Today he'd wanted to take Charlie on a drive to see the dinosaur exhibit at the Zoo. A drive through the rain wasn't exactly his idea of an adventure, though; and the boy would probably rather stay home to watch cartoons, anyway.

"Daddy!"

Dave looked to see the beaming face of his young son running toward him. With a bound, Charlie flung himself onto his father's lap. The two were soon tussling and wrestling.

"Hello, David."

Dave began tickling his son, smiling as the boy laughed and wiggled.

"Hello, Sarah. You're late."

"I'm sorry," replied Sarah, her eyes melting at the sight of the father and son wrestling on the bench. "We had a flat on the way here, and Frank had a few problems with the lug nuts. We ended up having to call a tow truck."

It figured, Dave smiled bitterly. Frank was great at being bossed around and saying "Yes, dear" to any woman within groveling distance. But the fool was useless when it came to doing anything productive. Even as an architect, the idiot seemed determined to prove himself a waste of Y chromosomes, preferring to work on art museums and government buildings rather than something useful, like a sports stadium.

"So where is he? I don't suppose you left him by the side of the road."

Stepping under the awning of the ice cream shop, Sarah took the seat beside her ex-husband. The misting rain had grown to a drizzle, and the darkening clouds promised more of the same.

"You make him nervous," Sarah said gently. "You always insult him, so he's in a foul mood for the rest of the day. He decided to wait in the car, so you couldn't make fun of him again."

Dave smiled bitterly: it was nice to know that he wasn't a failure at everything. He tickled his son again, laughing as the boy screamed with delight.

"You really shouldn't get him so wound up," said Sarah. "He's wound up enough already."

"We are having fun."

"And I was thinking," Sarah continued, looking down at the sidewalk. "You've had bad luck this month, as far as doing anything with Charles was concerned. Why don't you take him on the next sunny weekend we have? We can always readjust our schedule to even things out later."

"Aren't you being noble, today."

"David...."

"We'll manage," Dave said sharply.

"Well...think about it."

"We'll manage just fine."

"Give Mommy a hug?" Sarah sighed, and rose to go. Charlie threw himself into his mother's arms and squeezed as hard as he could. Sarah closed her eyes, and kissed the boy on the forehead.

"You have fun with Daddy," she smiled. "I'll see you Monday, right after school."

Watching Sarah dodge the puddles on the way back to her car, Dave took a deep breath. The autumn rain was falling steadily, looking to be with them for the next few days. Tussling the mop of hair on his son's head, Dave thought that in many ways, Charlie was the spitting image of his mother, with the same soft eyes and sweet smile.

"Okay, Squirt—what do you want?"

"Ice cream!"

"I think it's time for lunch. Let's get some bunny food over at the Supermart—and have some nice carrots for dessert."

"No! A hot dog, just like always!"

"I heard they were only going to serve cold dogs from now on, so they wouldn't need a stove."

"*Daddy!*"

"Let's go check."

Opening the door to the ice cream shop, Dave let his son race ahead of him. The hot dogs were actually good here. Too bad the ice cream was so pitiful. But it was Charlie's favorite. And it was the place Sarah and he had always stopped for lunch every Saturday, after taking the boy for a walk in the park.

Besides, Dave thought, he'd only gotten ice cream on one shoe today. The way his life was going, he'd need a matched set before the day was over.

Hunting Season

THE FULL MOON CAST SHADOWS through the leafless trees, and Willie sat down on a jagged stump. The cold air burned his lungs, and the rain washed the sweat from his face. He'd been running for so long he'd nearly forgotten what it was like not to hear the pounding of his heart.

The wind shifted to the east, and Willie heard the hounds baying in the distance. Rising to his feet, he kept moving west. On Dodge Lake there was a cabin that always stayed open through hunting season; if he could find it, he'd have someplace warm and dry to rest. The leaky old fishing boat the owner used for duck hunting should still be there. He could row it across the lake, down to the river and right into the State Recreation Area. Tripping over a tree branch in the dark, Willie felt a sharp pain crawling up his shin. The raw air made it hurt all the more. He swore at himself for being clumsy.

He didn't mean to hurt her, he thought, limping along the trail. In fact, there shouldn't have been anyone home, at all. Least of all that crabby old lady. He just wanted some easy money, and it was Bingo night at the church. He'd scouted the neighborhood for a month, and she was regular as a bowlful of prunes. Every morning, at precisely 10 o'clock, she took her little dustmop dog on a walk from her house to the park before stopping at the grocery store to buy the paper. Bingo was her one night out, and she never missed it.

At least, not for the last month.

At the crest of a small hill, Willie stopped to catch his breath. The hounds were closer now, just over Robbins Hill, a half-mile away. He could hear voices rising in the distance. He pressed on, the cold wind biting through his sweatshirt. His jacket would have helped cut the wind, though the fresh blood might have given the hounds a better trail to follow. He'd tossed it into a clump of brush when he first heard the dogs on his trail, hoping the mud and rain would confuse their noses.

Just shows how much you know about dogs, he sighed, pressing ahead.

Maybe if he'd killed the old lady's pesky dog right off: he always liked to keep the noise down to a minimum. It was a source of professional pride, he smiled grimly. And it might have been enough to keep her where she was, watching television, letting him back off to return another day when the house was empty. But the silver in the house was just waiting there, and he could still imagine what was locked away in the jewelry case he'd seen through the window, in the bedroom. With the price for silver heading skyward, it had been too tempting to pass up.

Behind him, he saw a ribbon of light glowing beyond the last hill. Flashlights, he thought. Probably made it a lot easier than groping through the half-darkness, tripping over every branch and downed tree in the woods. The cabin was just ahead, down the pathway through the trees and visible in the pale moonlight. He felt his heart pounding wildly. If he could just push himself a little more, he'd be safe.

What was it she'd screamed: not again...never again? Something like that. How was he to know she was a basket case who thought that every man was after her? It might explain why everyone in town thought she was such a strange old bird, always scolding the kids for stepping on her lawn, or the UPS driver for knocking too loudly on her door. It wouldn't help him now, of course, but next time he'd try to find out a bit more about the owner. It might help keep him from making another amateur's mistake. Like breaking into a house when someone was home.

Making his way down the path, Willie could hear the hounds baying up the hill. Breaking into a run he tripped over a woodpile at the end of the pathway. Rising at once, he limped madly toward the dock as the moonlight rippled over the water.

If she only hadn't come at him with that knife; he struggled to push the sight of her wild, fearful eyes from his mind. After all, what happened was really her fault: if she just hadn't rushed at him, screaming and slashing wildly. Then he wouldn't have had to defend himself. Once she'd drawn blood, he grabbed the first heavy object he could find. The baseball bat she kept by the back door was probably heavier than he needed, but he was too angry about being slashed in the face to think about stopping. After the first few blows, it probably didn't matter much anyway.

He saw the old fishing boat moored at the dock, and felt his fatigue melt away. Racing onto the rickety gangplank he worked frantically to cut the knots holding the boat in place. A garish beam of light flooded the shore, and he could hear men barking orders to him through a bullhorn. Pushing off from the dock, he fitted the oars into the oarlocks and began rowing as fast as he could toward the far shore, where the lake flowed into the river. He could feel his heart pumping harder with each stroke of the oars.

He never heard the gunshot. Soon his fading mind felt itself floating downward, into darkness. The last sensation he felt was the cold, enveloping his body.

*   *   *

"YOU'RE SURE it was him?" asked the sheriff.

The deputy looked up from his scope.

"Fine time to ask, Steve," he grunted, shaking his head. "But I knew him. Arrested him three times in the last three years. And I went to high school with him, besides. He was a loser then, and hasn't changed a bit."

Dropping the bullhorn to the ground, the sheriff took a deep breath and removed his two-way radio from his belt.

"Radio dispatch," he spoke into the walkie-talkie. "Tell them we caught up with him, but they may have to drag the lake to find him."

He knew the suspect as well, the sheriff sighed. He'd coached the kid in Little League. And a more promising young pitcher he'd never seen.

Lori Goff

LOVE

Love has no desire but to fulfill itself. To melt and be like a running brook that sings its melody to the night. To wake at dawn with a winged heart and give thanks for another day of loving.

Kahlil Gibran

LORI GOFF is a member of Ridgewriters. She resides in southeastern Oakland County with her husband, Wesley. She is the published author of two books, *Spirits Walking*—Stories of Appalachia and *The Heart of It All*— a book of prose and poetry. Her work also appears in the anthology, *Freefalling–Writing without Limits*, a how-to-write book.

Acknowledgments
The following works have been previously published:
Sunshine Angel, Satin Sheets, in *Freefalling* (iUniverse)
Wild Rose Memories, in *Spirits Walking* (iUniverse)
Love More, Elysian Fields, in *The Heart of It All* (iUniverse)

Finding Love in the Ruby Lo Pub

We loved with a love that was more than love.
                                    Edgar Allan Poe

Your lips like luscious red cherries, I kiss their
sweetness. I remember meeting you by chance

in the dim smoky Ruby Lo Pub in Chelsea after
friends wander off leaving the two of us alone

listening to *Strawberry Fields Forever* over and
over. While we listen to the song for hours we

secretly watch each other in hooded silence. Our
feet tap softly in sync to the music and our bodies

sway in unison. Your garland of flowers floats
on hair the color of taffy. If I could I would

whisk you away in Bacchus's chariot borne
by spotted king cheetahs to Nambia with the

speed of a supercar.

Sunshine Angel

Other men it is said have seen angels,
but I have seen thee and thou art enough.

George Moore

Elusive as the sunbeam
dancing in the wind.

Evanescent as the foamy
wings of the sea.

She was a bright silver ray
that warmed my path.

White heat with
a promise of heaven.

I tried to catch her song,
hold her still.

But there are spirits
not meant to be silenced.

A fleeting glimpse
of what was meant to be.

She slipped through my fingers
like water in a sieve.

Every time I thought
she was mine she was not.

Satin Sheets

At the touch of love,
everyone becomes a poet.

Plato

Satin Sheets
create a beggar
out of my being,
an endless search for
strokes of passion,
a yearning for
silken skin,
coolness for a
fevered brow,
escape from
fitted layers.

When Day is Done

Fire that's closest kept burns most of all.
                    William Shakespeare

Come sit by my fire.
A fire I made for you and mine.
Let the flames dance circles 'round us.
Let us feel the heat warm our hearts.
Let us watch fingers of flame flee.

Come sit by my fire,
when day is done.
Let us share this day's burden.
Let us dream together what tomorrow brings.
Let our clasped hands shelter yesterday.

Wild Rose Memories

We do not remember days,
we remember moments.
                    Cesare Pavese

Upon the barbed-wire fence
a tangled mass of greenery
weaves a curtain of pink.

A picture from childhood
fills my mind
of long ago fields, where

we ran through lavender-blue
sweet peas and dangled on low-
hanging apple tree branches.

I hold my breath hoping
to breathe the perfume
of forgotten memories.

My hand cups the bloom
as I inhale deeply;
heaven greets my senses.

Love More

For you see, each day I love you more
Today more than yesterday and less
than tomorrow.

Rosemonde Gerard

Today we cross a threshold together,
whisper our vows sealed with a kiss,
while bands of love circle our fingers.

Tomorrow will bring compromise,
no prize given for the victor,
only a bridge over ripples.

Fingertips will touch and part,
hearts will sing and sob,
love will win over.

One will give more,
one will take even more,
as one must love more than the other.

Elysian Field

Whatever our souls are made of,
his and mine are the same.

                    Emily Bronte

It all begins when night and day end.
I glide into the warmth of your heat.

Together feet and toes bestow kisses.
Hallowed and hollowed knees surrender.

Back and front sides settle in.
Your body nestles alongside mine.

Whispers of love cover us.
Weariness seeps away.

Wrapping arms engulf us
in a oneness of mastery and mystery—

heaven on earth when night reigns
and day awakens.

In the end—

nighttime brings solace and
daytime brings memories.

LOUISE GREENFIELD

LOUISE GREENFIELD says about herself: "Early in my career I sold many books and articles. I got burned out and quit. A peaceful ten years of painting and sewing followed. Then one day I lost my mind, my heart and all common sense and returned to writing. Alas! the world has switched over to e-kindle, and I am floundering around. I still write novels, but nowadays poetry is where my heart is."

Cruise to Belem, Brazil

WE TRAVELED TO BRAZIL in April of 1978, wanting to swing through the Amazon Delta and see firsthand what it was like. Knowing the ship would pass through the Equator my husband, Dave, and I thought long and hard about what clothing to take. Lightweight cotton, for sure. I bought some very lightweight cotton slacks, knowing that in some Latin countries women dressed in shorts were taken as an affront. With regard to a hat I found a straw hat that was so extremely lightweight that it was lighter than a feather.

The brochure stated that because the Amazon River was so full of huge hunks of debris, mostly sunken jungle trees, that it was dangerous for ships to pass through. Tour operators had a tough time persuading ship captains to go into the Delta because if the debris gets sucked into the ship's cooling system it becomes disabled.

Our cruise ship was The Jupiter of the Greek Epirotiki lines. The captain was a short, rotund Greek in white uniform and gold epaulets who was of a calm demeanor until we reached the Amazon. At that point, he went into a frenzy, staying awake day and night, pacing the pilot room, anxiously scanning the water, and chewing mightily on his cigarette holder.

We landed at Belem and were given four hours, from

eight to noon, to go on shore. It was our first land stop and everyone was excited. At that time Belem was a small city, and no buildings exceeded three stories in height.

We traveled with Dave's secretary, Irene, and her husband, Chet. Though an excellent secretary Irene dressed like a hooker at the office. On the day we left home to pick them up, Dave said, "I hope Irene is not wearing one of her usual get-ups." We were pleased to see that she wasn't; she wore plain slacks and blouse and a tailored jacket.

In those days on board ship you dressed for dinner every night, and of the two, her husband, Chet, was the dandy. He brought a steamer trunk, the old kind that "stood up" and was split down the middle so that, within, garments could be placed on hangers and arrive wrinkle-free. He dazzled us every night. He had packed four tuxedoes—white, black, dark blue, and maroon, plus a white linen suit, and pale linen slacks matched with a tan and white checked sports coat. Irene brought a mere two satin skirts and four dressy tops.

We went on shore at Belem . Within half an hour we felt the heat pressing on us, as if we had woolen blankets wrapped around us. My featherweight hat seemed like a brick on my head. After one and a half hours we went back to the air conditioning of the ship.

Buildings had central lobbies open from one end to another. At the shops salesclerks hung out in the doorways, going in only when a customer arrived. To handle runoff from the heavy rains, curbs were one foot high with gutters eight inches wide and twelve inches deep. You had to be very careful crossing the street lest you break an ankle in the gutter or fall forward and smash your nose, or both.

A colleague from work who was notorious for finding cheap trips had been to Belem and stayed at the Central Hotel. He asked us to take a picture. It was a plain white stucco building, with faint gray mold climbing up the exterior. To maximize air flow in the room, their windows went from floor to ceiling, heavy green shutters on the outside that could be pulled in and locked.

In the gift shops we saw beautiful carvings on very dark wood, mostly with a religious theme. Large crawling insects scuttled out of sight when a shopper touched something on a shelf.

Crossing the park we got hustled by a boy and girl for cigarettes. The boy, about sixteen, with pale skin and blond hair, looked exactly like an English Lord. Unfortunately he had very bad teeth. His girl friend was a mestiza. They told us how stylish they felt to be wearing jeans.

Determined to buy authentic Brazilian coffee two elderly ladies from the ship set out for the market, even though the tour guide advised against taking such a long walk. When they came back, wilting, they had to be rushed into an air conditioned room and ice bags placed on their foreheads.

When the shop passed the Equator there were ceremonies; the chef provided spun sugar decorations. The waiters were Greeks, very pleasant and attentive. They wore black pants, white shirts with full sleeves, and a broad red band at the waist. After having the same waiter for ten days, we naturally got friendly with him. Dave worked for Ford Motor Company and our waiter, Spyros, asked him for a recommendation for job with Ford of Greece. He told us he hated being away from his family for such long periods. Dave acquiesced. Later we received a telex from Ford of Greece saying Spyros had been accepted. We not only had a good time but we also did a good deed.

Hurly Burly

In the hurly burly of life
The marble-topped end table got stained,
Heirloom tablecloths got spotted,
Bathroom and kitchen sinks got chipped,
Boys jumped over the couch, it got lumpy,
We ate on the run, our figures got dumpy.

In the hurly burly of life
Kids went to college, checkbooks got thin;
Arthritis set in, fingers got stiff;
Glaucoma lurked, eyes got cloudy;
By the barrelful mistakes got made.
But we were useful, life got lived.

Sadness and anxiety got felt,
Yet in little pieces happiness got known.
(We are grateful it showed up at all.)
At this point, only one hope we've got –
that the hurly burly of life
carries on till the end.

Questions, Year 2000

Baby Boomers are awash with things.
Madison Avenue sold them a bill of goods
And then sold them the goods:
You can charge it, you can have it all.
Disdain parents who don't understand
And grandparents with funny accents.
At family reunions ignore them;
All you need to say is,
"Pass the potato salad, Grandpa."

Now Baby Boomers are reaching fifty.
Their houses bulge with electronics
Yet they feel their lives are rootless,
Suddenly they want to ask Grandpa questions:
"What little town in Russia were you born in?
Is it true you fled by night?
Why? Was the Czar's army after you?
Can we be proud of your struggles,
And thus of ourselves?"

Grandpa is in a nursing home, dithering.
He can't answer questions now.

KimberLee Bohley

KimberLee Bohley, a 1976 graduate of Walled Lake Western High School, has been writing poetry since she was fourteen years old. The daughter of Carl and Virginia Williams, she married her husband, Virgil, in 1977, and the two of them have four children. She attended Oakland Community College, where she was a featured reader at the OCC Auditorium in the 1980s. A past member of the Livonia Poets, she has been a member of Ridgewriters for the past three years.

Ivory Love

The ivory grew about
her white and slender neck.
Then where the humming birds
have pecked.
Left scars of love,
to her regret.
Twining then from head to toe,
this love sick vine,
where shall it go?
Hence
no blood
beats through her veins.
She is pale,
and shallow framed.
What was once in violent bloom
was in disguise
her ivory tomb.

Seasons of Love Are Timeless

We cannot meet in the fall,
 on the hill, among the marigolds.
Rocks that once lined our gardens, have fallen.
All is lost.
Tears we cried echo down streets of maple trees.
overhung, over grown,
gone to seed,
as we have.
On a chance that I might hurt you,
I have ceased to bloom.
Think of me at the smell of Lilacs,
and the touch of Sweet William.
For the fall has come.
Our love is falling,
twirling among brightly colored leaves
crumpled upon hardened ground.
The cool, cool, winds are crying.
I embrace the frost
Upon the hill
Among our marigolds,
Timeless.

Mother Blossoms the Daughter

Each bud,
Is our stepping-stone of love.
Each stem
The life line to our hearts.
Each Jagged leaf,
The past of which we overcome.
Each thorn,
The future of what's to be.
And tied with a ribbon,
My bouquet,
Is the mother.
Is the daughter.
With all their love
And it's pure worth.
Like a petal,
Pressed between pages of time
For always,
Forever,
And more . . . .

Rocking

The little girl is rocking,
in a chair, on the couch.
She rocks herself to sleep.
She rocks half of her life away.
But no one notices,
no one cares,
or feels.
Except maybe a slight breeze
from her rocking.
She rocks back and forth,
singing old songs to
her baby brother .
Her covers flutter
like angel wings.
Her hair tangles;
she cannot stop.
She rocks in any chair
she can find.
From a child to a teenager.
Friends find it amusing, comforting.
But mostly
no one notices,
no one cares,
or feels.
They just look the other way.
At adulthood,
the rocking does not cease.
The little girl is not gone.

She is still there,
on the chair or couch,
rocking.
Waiting for someone to notice,
to whisper it is all right,
to hold her with some love,
but it never comes.
Now the woman
creates her own comfort.
She rocks
with a steady rhythm,
a purpose.
Back and forth
back and forth,
singing old songs,
to her children.
And then
singing old songs to,
her baby grandson.
Yes,
she rocked most of her life away,
even though no one noticed,
she wouldn't have it any other way.

Your Longing Haunts Me Still

It comes to me in the night,
a summer night like this.
When mist has shadowed
part of the moon,
like a long sweet kiss.
In the vast twilight hours
it's searing hot with pain,
echoing at the edge of time
this frightening refrain:

And your longing haunts me still.

It comes to me in a moment,
from a distant time that's passed.
The when and where,
or who and what,
seems to never last.
Yet it's always there unseen,
just around the bend.
A love that could have,
should have,
had never really been.

And your longing haunts me still.

As I pull back the curtains,
within my fragile mind,
my heart fills with despair,

the soft and aching kind.
As I remember someone,
reach to brush my cheek,
wrenching from my tattered heart
a love that was so sweet.

And your longing haunts me still.

As thunder roars in the distance,
to a time that has long passed.
I beg for some forgiveness,
like a rose that cannot last.
I strain to see tomorrow,
blocking out the sun,
and strive for happiness
for you, the long lost one.

And your longing haunts me still.

Seeking Rainbows

I've been waiting.
Waiting for the sun to rise.
To break the dawn
and settle on the horizon.
I am looking for the light
to beam through
the prisms of my life,
and scatter little rainbows
on my carpet.
For you see,
this is where
my grandchildren dance
to a melody all their own—
my love.

KATHE FREUCHTENICHT

KATHE FRUECHTENICHT, author of the novels *Busua Pleasure Beach*, The *Translator, The Grimm's Secret* and the screenplay "Vienna Blood," was born in Jackson, Michigan in 1952. A graduate of the University of Michigan, she lived abroad in Europe and Africa in the 1970s. Kathe is the mother of three children and has two granddaughters. She lives with her husband in Farmington Hills, Michigan.

Acknowledgments
The excerpt from *The Translator* first appeared in the book of the same name, published by Publish America. The synopsis from *Busus Pleasure Beach* first appeared in *Clear Magazine*.

ELISE LAY RESTING COMFORTABLY in the feather bed in the stable, while Frederich busied himself puttering about with his automobile. There were so many repairs, it was dizzying.

The stone fences were crumbling, the holes from the bombs would take months to patch up, even the old rowboat on the lake was half submerged with water. Gone was the tender loving care which could only be administered by loyal employees, not just by Elise and Frederich themselves. Hof von Hohendorf, one of the most manicured, bucolic examples of the magnificence of the Hanoverian Kingdom, was becoming a shabby ruin, Frederich feared. Now that Elise's family fortune was in question, the wherewithal for maintaining the estate might have to come from other sources, but where?

"Colonel Cutcheons is coming out for dinner on Sunday. We plan to go hunting. Do you think you'll be up to receiving them?"

Frederich realized he was almost shouting to her, as he ambled back into the stables. The chill from the morning mist still clung to the old wooden plank floor, even though a fire raged in the mammoth fireplace. He missed the fine oak parquet in the main house and the delicate, ornately tiled stoves, but nevertheless was enjoying the fine June morning. Elise drew herself up out of the puffy mound of down comforter, enthusiastic that visitors were coming. She sorely missed the spontaneous concerts, which her guests usually persuaded her to give. It helped to no end to while away the tedious hours in the countryside, the lifestyle to which she was still not completely acclimated to. The *"Hausmusik"* warded off the restlessness, the longing for the stages of Frankfurt, Berlin and Munich. It all waxed an eternity away, that carefree life before the war, before Frederich and the baby. She knew she could never bring her father back from the gas chambers, but she considered herself lucky beyond belief that her mother and sisters managed to escape the death machine of the Holocaust. She desperately wanted to refocus her life on the future, but was still paralyzed from more than four years of exile within her own country.

"*Naturlich,* I'm going to be fine, really. Shall I make a cake? I have some jars of apricots left from last fall, I was saving them for company."

"Where is Frederich?"

"He was out playing by the lake, I told him not to go near it."

"Elise, you have to be more careful. He doesn't swim well yet." Frederich's stern demeanor sometimes made her tremble, but she knew he was right. Now that her sisters were gone, it seemed so much more difficult to look after him. It was a wonder she could keep up with him at all. She gathered her puffy comforter around her, warding off the chill of the June morning, and gazed out the filmy, soot-covered window. She spotted him playing contentedly in the grass marsh that made up a large portion of the lake's edge, pushing a small, red boat into the marshy water.

"Frederich, don't go into the water," she cried, trying to echo the same stern, razor sharp retort of her husband's, but coating it with her own softness. Her own childhood did not prepare her for the intimate relationship her son had with the natural world. She perused the length of the lake, mysterious with its mist-shrouded surface. This lake that saw the likes of Bach and Beethoven row upon it never failed to intrigue and charm her and she questioned whether her own son could appreciate the meaning of that genius and their close proximity to it. No matter what happened between she and Frederich, at least she was able to enjoy the enormous energy derived from a few years connection with that whiff of immortal possibility.

Synopsis of Three Novels
by Katherine Fruechtenicht

Busua Pleasure Beach

Busua Pleasure Beach is a coming of age novel that takes place in Paris and West Africa in the 1970's. Bethany McWhirter is a university student, photographing and chronicling West African artifacts in Ghana. Her family in Chicago, a divorced Bohemian mother and psychologist father, encourage her artistic exploration by first sending her to the Sorbonne in Paris and then on to Ghana, where the greater part of the novel occurs.

The liberal atmosphere of art school in Paris encourages the impressionable Bethany to apply for a Fulbright fellowship to help save for posterity, ancient Ghanian artifacts from the distant past.

At an isolated resort on a beach in Ghana, far from the pressures of modern life, she meets a motley group who will temporarily become her family. Eddie and Nancy, a couple fleeing the effects of Eddie's heroin addiction in New York City; a Ghanian boy named Kojo and his mother Adua; and Ananzi, a chieftain's son who was educated in England, make up Bethany's new-found circle of friends.

A near fatal bite from a poisonous fish, the loss at sea of Ananzi's father on the eve of a harvest celebration and clandestine ancient fertility customs become the lilting peaks and valleys of daily life upon Busua Pleasure Beach.

The climax of the story unfolds in the rape and planting of diamonds upon a naïve Bethany by a powerful Ghanian government official, bent on creating havoc with a military coup in Ghana. Following Bethany to New York City to retrieve the diamonds, Robert Akume, the government official, comes close to murdering her. A rescue by Nancy's uncle, a doctor from Brooklyn, saves Bethany. Sam, the doctor, falls in love with her free spirit and accompanies her back to Ghana, where she must choose between the doctor and his settled ways and the joyously youthful abandon of Ananzi, her African friend.

THE TRANSLATOR

YOUNG ELIZABETH HEDGES, an English volunteer in the NAAFI, the National Army and Air Force Institute, in June of 1945, goes to Germany to run a service club for British servicemen. Her boss, Colonel Bill Cutcheons, introduces her to Baron Frederich von Hohendorf, a friend and former schoolmate from Cambridge. Sparks fly between Elizabeth and Frederich, whose wife, Elise, an opera diva, has a Jewish family that has been devastated in the war. As the affair advances, Frederich's young son is mistakenly killed in the woods of their estate by German soldiers who refuse to surrender. In his grief, Frederich unleashes his passions for Elizabeth, who conceives a love child. He remains unaware of the baby and their short-lived relationship recedes into the background.

Meanwhile, Elizabeth's roommate, Lucy, becomes an unwitting target, drawn into the evil scheme of a former

German professor, who harbors hostility toward the Allied Forces. He abducts Lucy, whisking her away as a hostage to a defunct mine shaft in the mountains near Berlin, which doubles as a hiding place for escaping nuclear scientists from the Third Reich. Elizabeth and her boss, Colonel Cutcheons, team up with Chuck, a debonair GI, who leads them to the capture of the professor and the physicists. Thrown together in the course of the dangerous adventure, Elizabeth and her new GI friend, Chuck, find themselves in love. Elizabeth reveals her pregnancy, which Chuck nobly accepts, and near tragedy turns into joyous wedding preparations and a plan to live in the US.

Fifty years later, Elizabeth and her daughter, Sarah, an only child, journey back to Germany to attend a NAAFI reunion. Elizabeth senses the uncanny presence of Frederich, who is now near ninety, All the old passions stir within her as Sarah and Frederich meet and immediately understand the nature of their relationship. The Baron, having no other heirs, bequeathes his estate to a bewildered, but honored Sarah.

THE GRIMM'S SECRET

THIS HISTORICAL, FICTIONAL account of "The Grimm Brothers" takes place in Germany 1831, through the eyes of Dortchen Grimm, the wife of Wilhelm Grimm. The time period is before the birth of her third child, a daughter. Wilhelm and Jacob Grimm, the brothers, have been fired from their librarian jobs in their hometown Kassel and work as professors at the university in Gottigen. Their fairytale book, published in 1812, has made them a household name all over the world. Dortchen, a pious protestant, and Jacob, the older brother, find the mutual attraction between them too ardent to subdue and conceive a daughter. The three adults manage to live together with the secret, due to the unusual devotion between the two brothers. Wilhelm also concludes a twenty-year long friendship with Jenny von Haxthausen, whose highborn station in life rendered it impossible for them to marry.

Germany had been ravaged by Napoleon's yoke from 1806 to 1814. With his defeat, the fires of liberalism and a united Germany grew in the hearts of many inhabitants in all the separate principalities. The Grimm Brothers' gathering of oral tales represented a romantic, patriotic surge to salvage the ancient past and give it respectability, alongside the Roman and Greek, before it vanished. The Grimm Brothers devoted a lifetime of scholarship to give credibility to their culture and language in the eyes of the world.

Jacob and Wilhelm defied the orders of the new King of Hanover in Gottigen to renounce a liberal constitution created by the former king and are fired from their positions at the university and expelled from the country. All over Europe, "The Gottigen Seven" are praised for their heroic stance, but Jacob and Wilhelm return to Kassel for two years without jobs. Finally offered positions in Berlin at the Academy of Science, they became friends of the King of Prussia and celebrities throughout Europe. Wilhelm, Jacob, and Dortchen lived together in harmony for the rest of their lives.

Margaret Wilkie

MARGARET WILKIE grew up surrounded by stories and books. She finds learning to use the new-fangled devices in our new century a challenge, and is grateful to have patient grandchilren.

Acknowledgments
The writing of Margaret Wilkie has previously appeared in *Mr. Bellar's Neighborhood.com* and *Detroit Tourists*.

Strawberries

OUTSIDE THE BACK DOOR of the Grandville house was a sidewalk leading out back. Perpendicular to that sidewalk was a walkway leading to the garage. Nestled into the corner, surrounded by a low fence to remind the dogs to stay out, was a small kitchen garden planted with lettuce and such. Over the years as enthusiasm for gardening waned and shade grew, the strawberries took over.

They were day-neutral strawberries. I ordered 10 plants for my own garden and inevitably, since they came back year after year, some of the plants made their way over to Mother's house.

I don't know why they liked the kitchen garden so well that they spread all over, things did that in Mother's garden. The honey locust started out small, and later provided dappled shade over the whole garden. Maybe the dappled shade provided a nice environment for the strawberry proliferation.

The strawberries loved the spot, and took over in later years. The children used to pick lettuce and salad things for their dinner, first thing. Then they'd play and find strawberries. The good thing about day-neutral strawberries is that they produce during June for the main crop and then they keep on producing smaller amounts all summer with another flush in the fall. The pursuit kept the kids occupied, and rewarded, finding strawberries.

Mother liked to edge her beds with Fraise De Bois. She frequently noted, so that I think it is the last thing I will remember, that the small berries were a cultivated wild variety and came from the castle garden of Louis the 14th (let them eat cake, and apparently, strawberries).

When the kids finished searching the big strawberry bed, they moved onto the borders, looking for cultivated wild strawberries. The random nature of the hunt kept the children going back, as random rewards train better than regular, sure rewards. the search for strawberries also kept them away from the television , if only for a little while.

Sunday afternoons, mother insisted on tuning into the Shakespeare plays produced by the BBC that then were playing on public television. She didn't often watch them, since she was in the kitchen cooking and the television was in the den, but the kids did, even when they were young. They also played with the dogs or the tankful of guppies and tetras. They would explore what interesting things mother had left in the toybox.

One year, when we went away, Mother looked after the fish that belonged to the children. I do not recall how or why, but the fish stayed at her house. Later she bought a 20 gallon tank, as the fish had babies. The children loved to feed the fish when they visited and had to be shown to feed only a little and just twice a day, so that there wouldn't be too much food and the water go foul.

Populations of Tetras and Guppies went up and down in that tank. It was filled with small silver bodies when the kittens, who lived in the garage, visited. Besides the food that Mother put out for those kittens, their interests ran toward watching the fish in the tank.

I have often thought of that house in Detroit and the elemental growth of creatures there (including me). I wonder at the power of my mother to grow things, to allow them to grow. There be the secret, I think. Things want to grow, and mother knew to step aside and let them and pull out the weeds and compost the ones she didn't want.

Mother had a special talent—to feed what she wanted to grow and then step back and let growth take place. It takes faith to get out of the way, to let growing things grow where they will. It takes faith to understand and nourish life, life that seems to emerge from nothing.

No Longer in Charge

When I was young I was a conquering hero in the garden
I decided how things ought to go
being the most clever being around
I grew some pretty good stuff
spending time outside,
I began to understand that there are other forces at work
In the garden.
besides my spirit.

I am not the most clever
nor the best arbiter, orderer of things.
There are humming birds
and red bugs that eat the milkweed
who breed, lay their eggs on the milkweed
The red bugs are invasive and from Europe
After a few years
I see one once in a while and tut-tut them.
The first year those red bugs showed
They took over the tops of milkweed
and no doubt ate the monarch eggs
I wrung my hands,
I did not want them to take over
where the monarchs hatch

What it is that culled their numbers I do not know
something found them tasty,
or laid eggs on them, perhaps.

Things happen in the world,
one person cannot keep up with it all.

There are people who study ecosystems
Who recall the names of the red bugs
and know who eats them.
To them we owe honor and respect,
those biologists and ecologists

In my garden and in the world
There are powers in the shadows
ready to take their place on the great stage of life
The less over powering one does,
the more aware of the world
in all its beauty and heartache
one can become.

Future Thinking

You'll not know
What your father meant
What your mother meant

They spoke to you in metaphors
Because the young are loud and know so little
And the old care so much

Something they saw
something you will never see
they spoke to you and you thought understanding was
yours

History repeats itself
But we live in a new world

Holes in Jeans

I offered to sew up the holes in my daughter's jeans.
She bought them with holes, didn't want them patched.
It was then I knew that I was not ever to understand her
world.

Babies Say

Da Da Da Da
Sibilants (the start of Language)
Sibilants (they form at the lips)
Sibilants (making syllables)
Sibilants (child won't stop here)
Da Da Da
Sweet baby tells us
Da Da Da
Sweet baby sings
Da Da Da
Stirring hearts
Da Da Da

WALLACE CAMINSKY

WALLACE CAMINSKY was born in 1922, the first-born son of immigrant parents. After struggling through the Depression and World War II, where he served in the South Pacific, he finished college in 1947, graduating with a degree in English from Wayne State University, and was married the following year, soon to start a family of his own. Working for one of the Big Three automotive companies in Detroit, he wrote intermittently for the next twenty years, before embarking on a second career as a lawyer. He went to law school in the 1960s, and became an administrative law judge in 1975, serving in that position until his retirement in 1987. Always a voracious reader, his tastes in literature range from the short stories of James Joyce and P.G. Wodehouse to the novels of Charles Dickens, and the epic classics of Tolstoy...as well as the comedy of Monty Python.

Acknowledgments
The story "Three Birthdays" was first published in *All Fathers Are Giants and Other Stories*, a collection of short stories and poems by the author.

Three Birthdays

MY FATHER, WALTER PETROVSKY, was a dark, fierce-eyed Russian who didn't believe in God.

My mother, Anna Petrovsky, was small and gentle. A Polish-Catholic, she believed in God and prayed to Him often. Every Saturday night, lying next to her fierce husband, she would pray that my father would take her to church the next morning. Sometimes my father would snore loudly and pretend to be asleep. Or, if some anger was burning inside him that night, he would jump to his feet, roaring awful Russian oaths, his arms waving wildly until the rage was spent. Then he would lie down to sleep and let my mother go on with her prayers.

When Sunday morning came, she would put on her black velvet hat with the small rip in the veil, hang her big handbag over her arm and pause at the front door, her gentle eyes hoping that maybe this would be the day.

But Pop would be reading the editorial page of the Sunday newspapers, snorting and sneering at the stupidities he found there. Brusquely, from behind the paper, he would say: "Do not stand there Anna! Go! Your prayers did not work again!"

Sometimes he would put down his paper and look at her when he said it. Then a gentleness would come into his fierce eyes and his angry voice would grow soft. He did, after all, love my mother dearly, and wanted to be tender with her, but there was a principle involved, and when there was a principle, you had to be fierce. (Women never understood this in their men, he later explained to me; they chose to call it stubbornness or pig-headedness or other things that weren't nearly so nice).

But my mother loved her husband as well, and so whether he was gentle or not, she would sigh sadly, and leave him to his paper and his principles. There was always some sort of principle, it seemed. Oddly, though, his principles would change, or maybe just bend a little, with the birth of each new son. In the end, there were three of us.

Joseph:

MY BROTHER JOE was the first. I was ten years old when he left home, but I remember that he looked a lot like Pop. He was quiet and gentle, and he wanted to be a lawyer. He died on a forgotten island in the South Pacific.

When Joe was born, my parents were living with her father in a small town near the Baldwin Locomotive Works in eastern Pennsylvania. The old man owned a small grocery store near the railroad tracks. My father was supposed to be working at the store, but rarely did so because of his political activities. He was an active member of the Socialist Party, and on the night Joe was born, Pop was busy reciting some heroic Russian poetry to a party gathering. It was a matter of principle again. My mother, in the meanwhile, was busy delivering her son with the help of the woman next door—a fat, strong Polish woman who, as an added service, always brought a jar of home-distilled booze for the waiting males. In the days of Prohibition, she was the most popular mid-wife in town.

If not for the police, my grandfather would probably have polished off the jar all by himself. As it was, the town's constabulary raided the Socialist Party Hall just as my father's fervent, impassioned reading was bringing tears to everyone's eyes. This led to a mad scramble for the exits, but since most people were having trouble seeing through their tears, they kept bumping into one another and falling over the wooden chairs, tripping themselves and the police until everything was a confused, cursing tangle on the floor. In all the confusion, my father was actually able to finish reading his poetry—sustaining yet another principle—before making his escape. He ran all the way home, expecting a night stick on the back on his head at any moment.

Stumbling through the store to the living quarters at the back he collapsed, panting, at the kitchen table. His father-in-law, sitting in the chair across the table from him, was glaring red-eyed over the half-filled jar of booze. The old man filled his lungs to speak, forcefully and long, but just as he opened his mouth a freight train came rumbling by. The house shook, the half-filled jar of booze splashed around, and the old man's torrent of anger at his son-in-law was buried in all the noise. The son-in-law was about to reply in kind (for he had no doubt about what he would have heard...if he could have heard; and he did, after all, have his principles to defend), when the train was suddenly gone, clattering into the darkness, and in the quiet they heard the baby crying.

Maybe it was then, or maybe it was later when he went into the bedroom and saw his young wife lying in her bed in her father's house, nursing their first-born son, that Walter Petrovsky stopped being a socialist. He decided that he didn't want to change the world anymore; he just wanted to find a place in it.

Stanley:

I WAS THE second son. Joe was twelve when I arrived; my mother was thirty-five, and my father was thirty-eight.

The family was now settled in Hamtramck, an enclave surrounded by the big city of Detroit and coming back to life after the bleakest years of the Depression. Factory whistles were blowing again and the men were starting back to work.

It was about this time that my mother began her conversations with God. As a matter of fact, she half-believed that the two of them had come to an agreement about ending the Depression. She was a little puzzled about why He couldn't do anything about her husband's church attendance, but at least she didn't have to go to church alone anymore.

Every Sunday, when the bells sounded from St. Florian's, Joe would escort his mother to the church a couple of blocks away. And a couple times a week—to show that he wasn't taking sides—when the thump of the plants had stopped for a shift change and the factory whistles signaled that it was time, he'd walk down the street in the opposite direction to meet Pop striding home from work, and carry his lunch pail home for him.

My father was working steady now, and he contemplated the future with high hopes. He decreed that his next-born child would have the advantages of pre-natal doctor's care and a hospital delivery.

Since I was the next-born child, this was all fine with me. It also added considerably to my status later on, since our neighborhood boasted of very few hospital babies. But for my mother it was a ghastly experience, and one that left her a shaken woman.

She was appalled at how thorough a doctor's examination could be.

"And they looked like such nice, young boys," she would say, shaking her head sadly at the thought of what education could do to a person's morals. Partly because of the doctors, she decided that she would never become pregnant again.

But probably the biggest reason for her new-found interest in family planning was that she just thought it unseemly for a woman over thirty-five to be with child. In her old-country village, people of that age were considered old, and treated with the respect due one of the elders. She concluded that it simply wouldn't look right for her to be pregnant anymore. Though she knew the church might bless the act that caused it, the fact of pregnancy was growing evidence of funny business afoot, and she didn't want people to know that something like that was still going on in her house. But she had problems explaining the nuances of the Church's thinking on the subject to her husband.

"Rhythm!?" he roared. "Rhythm is for the orchestra!"

And for a long time after my arrival, my father and his principles were consigned to living a monk-like existence. Maybe that's why he could always terrify me with his rages. Instinctively, like any good Catholic boy, I suspect I always felt guilty.

Ladislaus:

LADDY WAS OUR family's third son. It was 1939; I was seven years old when he was born. And my mother still hadn't changed her mind about doctors.

Laddy started making his presence known on the last day of August. It had been a hot day, but also a wistful day, a sad kind of summer's-almost-over day, one that made little boys complain that Labor Day was coming too early this year, and left their fathers to wonder how many more good years they had left, themselves.

A fresh breeze came with the twilight, promising a cool night. But most of the narrow, crowded houses were still stuffy and warm, so the people—one by one—left their dinner tables to relax on the back steps. The women, shapeless and bulky in their big aprons, stood on the porches, wiping thick hands in their dish towels; the men sat on the steps, a garden hose in hand, religiously wetting down the gently tended green of their tiny backyards. One or two radios were on. There was some trouble about Danzig, it seemed, and people thought there might be news.

Mostly it was quiet. The old country people whispered in their own special language, their round and early Polish sound rising like sad and gentle murmurs. The murmurs all stopped whenever the music on the radio came to an end, but resumed when everyone realized it was just a commercial.

The breeze that evening came from the darker part of the sky. It soothed the trees that crowded into corners between fence and garage, shading the trash cans and sending their roots deep under the alleys.

I was sitting next to my brother Joe on the back steps, listening to the rustling leaves. It made me think of the smoke that hurt when it touched the eyes, and of fires that made the alley bright, flickering along the whole block. And that made me think of our drives out to the country, where Pop bought bushels of green tomatoes and red tomatoes and hot peppers and cucumbers and apples. For nights afterwards, the house would be filled with the smell of cooking and canning.

"Will we go to the farm soon, Joe?"

"I don't know. Maybe."

We hadn't done much of anything through the summer. There had been one trip to Belle Isle, and we'd had to come back early then because my mother had gotten sick. And we hadn't gone to see a single Tiger's ball game. Joe was working at the Dodge Plant through the summer, earning money towards his tuition at college, where he was a sophomore, and for some reason my father didn't seem interested in baseball anymore.

"Is Ma sick, Joe?"

"No, Why?"

"Pa's always talking about doctors. Why is he always talking about doctors?"

Joe looked at me for a while and then hugged me around the shoulders.

"Ma's going to have a baby. Pa wants a doctor to make sure she's all right."

"And the hospital?"

"This baby is going to be special, like you."

We sat quietly for a long time, not moving. The whispered talk of the neighbors seemed reverent and hushed, like talk in a hospital, or funeral home, or bank.

"Will it be soon, Joe?"

"Pretty soon, I guess."

A radio said something about the Prime Minister of England sending a message to Hitler. During the announcement, everything seemed very still. After it was over, it seemed like the whole city was sighing.

"Will there be a war, Joe?"

Joe was about to answer, when we heard loud voices from the house. We stood up and, through the kitchen door, we saw my mother run into the bathroom and slam the door shut. Then Pop started pounding on the door and roaring her name.

"Pa, what's the matter?" Joe called

Pop burst through the door and stood on the porch, staring wide-eyed and breathing rapidly.

"It's her time!" he yelled. "It's her time and she won't go!"

"What do you mean, Pa?"

 For a long moment, he could only manage some half-strangled Russian sounds, and then he blurted out: "By herself, she says! By herself!"

I started blubbering, and then I started to wail. My father slapped his hand against his forehead and rolled his eyes up towards the dark sky.

"We got ourselves enough trouble, little Stanley," he shouted, "without your singing! Go next door and get Mrs. Sielenski. And Joe, you go get the doctor."

I ran next door. Mrs. Sielenski had heard and was already tying on her babushka when I knocked. She was very round and her fingers were like little sausages. "Oy-oy-oy," she whispered as she hurried her hard-to-move body.

The bathroom was next to the kitchen. When I got back with our round and worried neighbor, my father was at the locked door, pleading with his wife.

"Anna," he said gently, "Please don't be foolish. Come out so someone can help you."

He was so gentle and soft in his tone that it frightened me, and I started to wail again. I thought my mother was going to die. Pop glared at me and rolled his eyes up again.

"Anna!" he shouted; and then, remembering, he softened his voice. "Anna, please be a good girl. Mrs. Sielenski is here to help you."

Mrs. Sielenski's sausage-shaped fingers fretted along the corner of her apron.

"Oy-oy-oy!" she sing-songed over and over. "Oy-oy-oy!"

My father raised his arms and slapped them to his sides. Then he glowered at the frazzled neighbor lady.

"'Oy-oy-oy,' I can do myself," he roared. "That's not why I want you."

"Oy-oy-oy!"

I wailed louder. Pop was disgusted with both of us and turned back to the door.

"Please, Anna."

My mother's strained voice came through the door.

"It is too late for that now, Walter. You'll just have to wait."

A police siren sounded. It started on the other side of town, came up Joseph Campau and kept coming closer and closer, swelling bigger and bigger, filling the street, and finally slowing down and dying in front of the house. The front door was thrown open, and it sounded like a crowd was stomping through the house, heading towards the kitchen. It was Joe with a doctor and two policemen. My father grabbed the doctor.

"Help, Anna," he said. "She's having a baby."

"Of course," the doctor said crisply. "That's what I'm here for. Where is she?" Pop indicated the bathroom door with a nod of his head.

"Well, ask her to come out, please, so we can get on with it."

Pop's eyes bugged out, his neck corded up, and two gigantic veins popped out on his forehead. "What the hell you think I'm trying to do!" he bellowed.

"Shall we break down the door, doc?" one of the policemen asked.

"You can't do that, Basil," the other one protested. "You'll scar the kid for life!"

"You are the doctor," Pop yelled. "You tell us what to do."

"Oy-oy-oy!" said Mrs. Sielenski.

The doctor thought that there might be too many people in the house and asked everyone but Mrs. Sielenski and Pop to leave. Joe took me out on the front porch and we sat down on the porch swing. The two policemen chased away the small crowd that had gathered around the squad car, and then they sat on the steps and lit cigarettes.

"What time you got?" Basil the policeman asked Joe.

Joe looked at his wrist watch.

"Eleven-thirty."

"Hope this don't take too long. We get off at midnight."

Joe rocked the swing lightly and tried to settle me down. It took a long time, but he finally did. "Ma is going to be fine," he said. "You'll see."

"I was scared."

"Sure you were. So was Pa. So was I. But the doctor's here now. He'll make sure nothing bad happens."

One by one, the lights in the houses down the block had gone out, but no one was sleeping. All the radios were still on.

"Did you hear the news?" one of the policemen asked Joe.

"No."

"The Germans have their soldiers all along the border. They could move any time now. Unless somebody chickens out, it looks like there's going to be a war."

We waited. The swing squeaked and stopped, squeaked and stopped. Far away, the big Stamping Plant thumped, pumping like a gigantic heart.

I got sleepy. My eyes grew heavy and I felt very tired. I must have dozed because I didn't hear my father come out on the porch, and only half-heard him when he sat down on the swing.

"It's all right. Mama's all right, that crazy woman. You got a brother. Oy, that crazy woman of mine."

My father picked me up and carried me into the house. "Look, Stanley—look!"

With great effort, I opened my eyes and looked. There was Mrs.. Sielenski, a fat, round smile straining against the babushka, cradling a bundle in her big arms. The bundle looked like a red monkey and didn't really interest me.

"You were really wonderful, Mrs. Sielenski," the doctor said in kinder voice than he'd used before. And Mrs. Sielenski's head bobbed with pleasure and her smile spread even further. She walked off with the baby into the bedroom and left him there with my mother.

My father was still carrying me as he walked out with the doctor. The two policemen were still there.

"What time is it , doc?" asked Basil.

"Twelve-thirty."

"That's not too bad. We'll be home by one."

"How's everything?" the other asked.

"Fine," the doctor answered.

"The lady okay?"

"Uh-huh. And the boy too."

The three of them walked to the squad car and climbed in. Basil, who took the seat behind the wheel, stuck his head out the window before driving away.

"By the way," he called back, "the radio says the Germans have marched across the border." Waving, he pulled away.

It was very dark and there was a chill in the air. The breeze freshened and moaned, going between the houses. Pop carried me back into the house and held me in his arms. His cheek was sandpaper rough, and he smelled of tobacco.

From a long sleepy distance, I heard my father and Joe talking about the war. And I felt my father's arm tremble slightly. Even then, half asleep and seven years old, I knew that the little red monkey would be his last son. Summer was over, and soon the world would begin to die.

An Inconvenient Tomorrow

BILL COLLINS, A SCI-FI author and internet science editor, woke up on Sunday morning and knew that the world would come to an end in two days.

His wife, Ann, was still asleep as he eased out of bed.

He went to the window to study his backyard while he puzzled over the knowledge he'd been burdened with. There was the dead apple tree, brown dead grass, frail dying bushes near the fence baking under a hot relentless sun. It didn't rain anymore and the yard was dead, he mused. Most of the country was turning to dust and the oceans were claiming more and more of the coastal areas. It was as though the earth had gotten sick of the infestation of humans (they were like maggots) and was taking steps to cure itself of the disease. Maybe this had happened before. Time and life starting over and over again, trying to get things right. Big Bang after Big Bang.

Ann stirred in the bed, yawned loudly and stretched out her arms. He wondered: does she know? She looked at him and a slight, tentative smile touched her lips. She sat up, still looking at him, gave a little shrug and stood up. Maybe she knows, he thought and shrugged back. Then they embraced for a long minute. They could hear their twelve-year old son stirring in his room. What was coming was not to be discussed or even acknowledged, especially to the young.

Chris came into the kitchen while his parents were having a second cup of coffee. He was wearing his Tiger baseball cap which still had the English, D even though the team's ball park had long ago moved to Lansing, and he was pounding his fist into the baseball mitt he was wearing. His expression was very, very serious and he tripped over the throw rug in the doorway. He was a handsome boy, Bill mused, he must have got his looks from Ann. He came to the breakfast table still wearing his baseball glove. Noticing his father's quizzical frown, he reacted loudly saying, "I'm breaking it in!" He doesn't know, Bill thought, wondering whether or not to be relieved.

Ann told him to take his cap off as she brought his cereal to the table. Bill studied him thinking, "This is my son. I'm supposed to take care of him." And he grimaced.

"What would he have looked like grown? His eyes, his height, his hair? What would he have done? What could he have accomplished? I was supposed to help him. This is my son and I failed him." He shook his head thinking: Don't think about it. Don't think about it.

Ann nudged him.

"Chris is trying to get your attention, dear."

"I'm sorry Chris. I was day-dreaming. What's up?"

"Can we play catch later? I need to get some practice."

"Well sure we can but what's wrong? Are you having trouble at team practice?

Chris gave an exasperated sigh and said, "I think I'm good but I don't think the coach likes me. He never puts me in the game until the game is almost over."

He pounded his fist into his glove. "And he won't let me pitch!"

"Well let me look through the paper first, okay?"

Chris nodded and said he'd meet his father outside. Bill took up the paper which wasn't more than five or six pages. Newspapers had been shrinking in size due to the chronic shortage of paper which was tied to the diminishing forests.

"Do you want part of the paper, Hon?" Bill asked.

She shook her, "If there's anything important you can tell me about it." She cleared the table and then asked him, "Do you want to go to the zoo today? I heard the Polar bear has revived a little."

"Sounds like a good idea. The only news worth reporting is that the volcanic activity in the Pacific has slackened off. Great news, eh?"

THEY TOSSED the ball back and forth easily. Chris moved with a sort of awkward little boy grace. He's a natural, Bill thought.

"Let me pitch a little bit," Chris yelled. So he wound up, imitating some big league pitcher, and threw a fast ball with fair accuracy and bite. His delivery was a smooth three-quarter side arm. And then he threw a ball that curved.

"Where did you get that pitch?" Bill asked.

"I just read about how the pros hold the ball before the throw it", Chris said proudly.

"Well, you better not throw it too much. You might hurt your arm. Wait till you're...whatever.

After a while, they took a break on the back porch and Chris mentioned that he'd seen pictures of ball parks and they all had green grass. What happened to the green grass he wanted to know.

"The weather changed", Bill said huskily, it got hotter."

"Well, will it change back?"

"Sure, sure," Bill said. "Maybe it will. But for now, we should get into the house for a while. It's feeling kind of hot."

At the door, Bill paused and said, "Your mother thought we could go to the zoo after lunch. Sound good?"

"Sure" Chris said, "sure."

THE ZOO WAS in Royal Oak north of Detroit. Detroit's name was on the zoo's water tower. That city had once been the largest city in the State but once the river which ran by Detroit had turned into a widening, deepening lake which covered the tall buildings for several stories, it was abandoned and the city with the zoo became the state's biggest city. Driving to the zoo, you could still see the top of the big buildings through the rear window.

"Lot of people going to the zoo," Bill noted. There was a slight delay getting into the parking lot, but there weren't any workers collecting parking fees. Why should there be? Bill thought.

Most of the crowd consisted of families with young children. Fathers and mothers walking together, sometimes holding hands. They were all watching their children Bill thought, not guardedly but almost wistfully. The children were interacting with their peers, laughing at nonsense, mugging one another. Chris found a baseball fan and they were arguing about who was the best Tiger and whether the team would go to the World Series. There weren't many old people around; they were staying home.

The zoo's better days were far in the past. The small train that used to take visitors to the outskirts of the grounds was long out of service. The exhibits that featured meadows for gazelles, deer, and antelope had turned weedy brown (just like my yard, Bill thought) and the animals were gone. Some lions and tigers were housed in exhibits that had rocks and concrete cliffs with a little water. And there was the polar bear exhibit featuring the last surviving bear. It looked sick and forlorn. Chris wanted to know why there no more bears.

"They lived on the ice up North and the ice disappeared."

"How come?" Chris asked.

"The weather changed."

How come? Bill thought, how come? Maybe way out there, there's this bratty galactic kid whose playing games with us and now he's bored and tired and he's shutting everything down.

Walking around the zoo brought more evidence to Bill's mind of the mischief of this spoiled brat he had envisioned. Dying animals, algae-infested water, brown grass, and people walking around like sleep walkers except for the kids, and even they were slowing down as the daylight started leaking away.

"Time to start home, Bill?", Ann asked.

"Yeah, yeah, I guess so."

*   *   *

ON THE WAY home, Bill fumed about his evil galactic brat. "He's messing us all up," he muttered. "He's interfering with my function as a father. Fathers are giants, they mold the future, they produce the star scientists, the effective politicians and...and Yes!—the star pitchers!"

"What are you mumbling about, Bill?" Ann asked.

"Fate."

She sighed and stroked his cheek as they pulled into their driveway. It was Six o'clock. That brat's idea. Bill was thinking, was to make sure we knew it was our fault, so that grown-ups would feel guilty and the kids were spared the knowledge of the end of time and adults would be burdened with the task of pretending that everything was "swell": schools, stores, sports....

THEY HAD A light supper of sandwiches and soup, then watched the baseball game. The Tigers were playing in Harrisburg and they lost to the Yankees 7-5.

"They didn't care," Chris complained and went to his room to do his homework. Bill was still brooding about his galactic bête noire. They or it wanted to saddle us with a sense of guilt about how we'd treated this planet, about how we bequeathed our kids nothing. They or it wanted us to know that Time was out. No yesterday, no today. No tomorrow; keeping it from the kids so that we would know what they'd lost but they wouldn't, which was why there would be school tomorrow.

He swore under his breath. Ann heard him, took his hand, kissed it and said, "We blew it." It startled him that she seemed to be on the same guilt trip.

"I guess we did," he said and leaned over to kiss her. "You going to the office tomorrow," she asked?

"No," he said smiling ruefully, "We're taking the day off."

MONDAY MORNING the radio alarm went off with the metallic voice calling for another hot day with no rain and plenty of smog. The stock markets were closed worldwide and all local courts were closed. There was to be no mail delivery.

Bill and Ann woke up at the same time and, from the clatter of dishes, they could tell that Chris was already in the kitchen getting his cereal.

"Hold off, big guy, wait for us," Bill called.

In the kitchen, Chris was gulping down his cereal, wearing his baseball cap and with his mitt next to him.

"What's the big hurry, sport?"

"I don't know why but the bus is coming early today and don't forget I'm going to baseball practice today. I think there's a game scheduled for tomorrow."

"Pick you up after practice? Bill asked.

Chris frowned and said, "You never pick me up after practice. I always walk home with Pete. Why would you pick up today?"

Bill slapped his head. "Of course," he said, "I just forgot."

Chris got to his feet and headed out the door. "See you when I see you", he shouted and slammed the door behind him.

Bill looked at Ann, smiled and said, "I thought he'd never leave."

She smiled back, took his hand and lead him to the bedroom.

*   *   *

MOST OF THE morning was spent in bed. Just before lunch, they showered. The radio was on, the weather hadn't changed.

"Do you think we should go to church?" Ann wondered.

"No," Bill said. "Let's just go for a little walk. Maybe later, we could go to the ball field and watch Chris at practice."

"No," Ann said, "You know he doesn't like us watching him. It makes him nervous. We better not."

"Right," Bill said. "So lets just walk." Nothing different, he thought.

There were others on the sidewalk. They were couples, a lot of them holding hands: quiet, somber, attentive to time. Passing one another, they exchanged greetings: good evening, or peace, or have a nice day. The last was usually accompanied by a sheepish smile.

As they walked, the day was changing, the light ebbing away, the sun weakening. "Let's go home and listen to some music," Bill said. Music was coming out of many of the houses they passed: soft music, quiet music, some church music. They went home, turned their entertainment center to music and held each other on the sofa, exchanging an occasional kiss. After a while they both dozed off.

Ann woke up first. "What time is it?" she asked anxiously, "Shouldn't Chris be home?" Bill checked his watch, it was almost five o'clock but the light was fading fast. There won't be much of the day left Bill thought and went outside to watch for Chris. After some minutes, he saw him a few blocks away walking with his friend; except he wasn't walking, he was hopping, spinning, waving his arms. His friend turned off a block away and then Chris saw his father. He came running towards his father, his eyes wide, his mouth open with a happy smile while shouting,"Dad! Dad!" He ran to his father, caught his breath and shouted "Coach said I could pitch tomorrow!"

Tomorrow! The word exploded in his mind and he turned away from the smiling face to glare skyward, swearing silently at the galactic brat.

LOUIS GARVER

LOUIS GARVER is a long-time resident of Redford, Michigan. Among his many essays and poems is "The Anson Anthology," a collection of memories and impressions of life in small-town Michigan.

from **The Anson Anthology**

Introduction
All this happened,
if it happened,
a long, long time ago.

I say if it happened.
No two people see ,
the same event
the same.

And some things
never happened.
They are made up
of the whole cloth.

And yet they
could have happened.
In fact did happen,
not in the way depicted.

There is no town
called Anson on the
map of the State of Michigan
It is a name made up.

But—there is a town,
a living, robust town,
More vibrant and admired,
than sixty years ago.

We will not sneer
or deride this town.
We tell our stories
out of pride.

And if it seems
Otherwise to you–
Well mores
were different then.

If some child says,
"it never happened."
Why they are right.
it never, never happened.

We can not, will not,
visit on their heads,
the folly of their
fathers.

If we keep alive,
the hoary tale
of legislators
renting hacks,

And taking fast women
From Lansing to the
hotel– well what did
you expect?

That was a hundred
years ago.
They didn't
have motels.

But fifty years ago,
It was the moralest
of towns
In a very moral age.

The Killing
Every town has its killing,
At least one if not more.
It has to happen on Main Street,
No matter the name of the street,
Washington, Lincoln, whatever...

And it has to happen in broad daylight.

This killing is so old that
There may be more recent killings.
Probably are, as I say,
The town is the county seat,

And has been around...
For a hundred and seventy years.

So Anson is an old town,
And I am old too.
If I left more than sixty years ago,
And this killing occurred long
before that...

Certainly my details are sketchy.

You can write your own scenario.
A jealous husband, the town policeman,
Suspicion of an illicit affair,
A confrontation on Main Street...

There had to be a killing.

Only the details are interesting.
That a man armed with a shotgun,
Came at a man walking with his wife.
The cop shot him dead with his pistol,
Right there in broad daylight...

What's wrong with this picture?

How does a man with a pistol holstered,
beat a man with a loaded shotgun?
The sheriff found nothing amiss,

The cop exonerated, but some of the
people, said the man was murdered...

On the main street of Anson.

Resolvo Greene

"Resolvo Greene, Resolvo Greene!
My goodness, my man where have you been?
You came early this morning to fix my light,
You left for a part, now its almost night.
Where have you been?"

The widow Ferribly was asking the question.
His look in reply showed no comprehension.
He thought for a minute, but didn't reply.
You had to be patient if you hired this guy.
Yet he was smart.

His children were brilliant at Michigan State.
Each and everyone of them proved to be great.
His son, Clive, Editor of *State News*.
The best there was they said of his views.
He went straight to a big city paper.

Resolvo scored highest on his license exam.
You wanted the best? He was your man.
You wanted the best? It was a great bounty,
The best electrician in Ingham county.
Brainwise, that is.

Still, he made you wait and fuss and fidget,
Some people called him the village idiot.
He didn't charge much, and I wonder,
Maybe that was his greatest blunder.
We will never know.

Herbie Boatwright
In the end they found him guilty.
Killed his mother-in-law by slow
poison. The prosecutor's case was
weak. But they nailed him anyway.

Of course the town divided. Old
ladies loved the boy as much as
he was hated. Old lady Irwin
was the tightest bitch in town.

Herbie dearly loved the dollar, he
spent too much, lost too much, lost
other people's money. He moaned down at
the bar, the old lady refused him,
even the price of a new Chevy.

She died. Buried. End of story.
But Herbie spent, new Packard, trap gun,
Leica, new blonde in Lansing. Murmurs.
They dug her up. Slow poison.

He should have beat the rap. But juries
hate a guy like Herbie, hard-scrabble farmer
juries, hate powdered, perfumed, soft handed
jerks like him.

We guys down at the bar, think he could
have beat the rap, if he had just laid
low and bought a beat up Chevy.

Geraldine Wiggins
Geraldine Wiggins.
Ask her if there is life after high school?
I saw her standing alone at our Senior Prom.
I asked Stanton to dance with her.

Next day she quit.
Apparently she'd had enough,
of stuck-up, snobbish
Anton High School.

I saw her next year.
Pregnant with an inner beauty,
and then no more I saw her
on the streets of Anson.

Years later, my mother
told me her story. A no
good bum of an older man
married her to get to her mother.

He got his chance,
He ditched her for her mother.
My mother hated that woman
and that bum.

Geraldine lives in Arizona.
She remarried, and I hope,
now has a decent life.
Ask her, is there life after high school?

Would she say—yes, yes, doubly yes.
At least I hope she would.

Hard-Ass Harry Parma

Harry Parma, civil engineer,
Stern, Humorless,
Took it out on his wife and kids.
His road crew called him
"Hard Ass Harry".

His wife, a nurse, matched him
In brains and determination.
Had two smart sons, one a PhD,
The other a civil engineer.

Some time after age forty,
Harry took sick of pneumonia.
Drowned in the bathtub.

Authorities never questioned,
No autopsy, inquest, nothing.

But small towns are small towns.
The whisper story: his wife held his head under water.
Till he drowned.
She never was queried.

You say, "It couldn't happen today.
It would be investigated."
Don't be too sure,
If nobody cared,
Who would be there to press charges?

But don't believe everything
You read in these pages.
Typical small town story,
Typical Americana.
Perhaps it never happened.

If we believed every urban legand,
Of the wife who did in her husband,
There would be no room in the graveyard,
For all of the men,
Who died of natural causes.

Frieda Fletcher
Lived on a farm,
Just outside of town.
Big hearty gal, whose face and clothes were awfully plain.

Unlike her cousin Millie, who was "Miss Personality".
Why not–her dad was mayor,
while Frieda's folks farmed.

In high school Frieda
had no dates. After that
they sent her to Moody
Bible School, just outside Chicago.

Some girls just went to work.
But old-money Methodists
sent their girls to Albion.
They were enrolled at birth,
it must have cost a lot.

The Calvinist went to Alma,
some others out of state.
Millie to Milwalkee Downer.
-why I do not know.

Frieda's folks were religious,
more than most I guess.
Frieda was a quiet girl,
smiled, laughed a lot.
But not so much you'd notice.

One time her folks refused,
to let her attend a dance.
Frieda took a hammer and smashed
every window on their old car.

The Chemist
We call him the chemist,
because that is what he was.
If we name names someone may be hurt.
Child, grandchild– who knows?

Does not seem possible,
After 50 years anyone
would know. Ah, but you do
not know your small towns.

If we wrote about the banker,
who had his fancy girlfriend,
(I think she may have run one
of the local beauty spots)

While he maintained one of the
most respected facades in
town. And no one faulted her,
she was beautiful and discreet.

But a drunk–good heavens,
what a disgrace! Hush, don't

mention it. As we say,
Even unto the fifth generation.

So the chemist was a drunk.
He did not frequent,
the lowlife dusty bar.
He drank at home.

As did all the respectful people.
Their liquor, beer and wine
delivered to the back door.
Prohibition never ended.

Which makes you wonder,
we didn't know. His wife
divorced him, kicked him out,
the plant may have fired him.

He left town–that should be
end of story. But it is not.
There is more. My father, a
drinker, thought his wife nuts.

My father thought him,
a connoisseur of wines.
A man of refined taste,
Much like himself.

They never drank together,
or mingled socially.

Down at the plant, my father
a compounder, he a chemist.

So we lost track of him.
Life goes on. Years later
I met his wife at a big fund
raiser for the Republicans.

She was checking coats.
Had a state job, lowly, I
am sure. Had to volunteer
for the fund raiser.

Told me the chemist was a
drunk living in Detroit,
on the Cass Corridor,
a hopeless helpless alcoholic.

Strange world, a chemist,
an exalted human being,
doing research on folic acid,
how could he have fallen?

Living in an idyllic place
and time. Small town, small
plant, looked up to, respected.
How could he have fallen?

On My Surgery
(or I give myself permission to be a very bad poet)

If I should die, grieve not for me,
remember it was meant to be,
God willed it.

But rather pity my poor wife,
through all the years of toil and strife,
six children.

Child bride until my orders came,
then navy wife, she was dead game,
to go with me to Long Beach.

All things, all times, we've been together,
in sunny clime or coldest weather,
for nearly 50 years.

If I should die, don't weep for me,
Rather let my children see,
I had good friends.

I leave them nothing tangible,
for what I have I must it will,
to their mother.

She will be "well fixed", they say,
And if she wishes, as she may,
Give everything to them.

There, you all about me know,
I'll leave them books and guns and bow,
It's called a heritage.

If I should die, then pray for me,
A life in heaven I can't see,
without my wife, Joan.

If I can but a bargain strike,
I'll stay in limbo or the like,
'Til we go in together.

BETTY RUDDY

BETTY RUDDY lives in Birmingham, Michigan. She holds an MFA in writing and literature from the Bennington Writing Seminars. Two of her essays, *Motherless,* published in *Fourth Genre,* and *The Shark's Jaw,* published in *The Journal,* were named Notable Essays by *Best American Essays.*

Acknowledgments

A slightly different form of this essay was published in the May-June 2004 issue of *FosteringFamiliesTODAY.*

Second Violin Mother

I HAVE BECOME ACCUSTOMED to the quiet in this childless house. No evening quarrels over bedtime or homework; no teenage reveling to keep me awake. I admit, though, that I miss the pile of young boy bodies at the kitchen table on sleepover mornings, and their polite voices clamoring for pancakes and bacon. I miss the clutch of teenage girls who used to muse over the caloric content of each item in my well-stocked pantry, all the while munching on chips and candy. I miss, too—although it seems crazy in light of the chaos at the time—those days ten years ago when my two pre-teen children, Katie and Walter, were joined by two toddling foster brothers, Randall and George.

None of these children are here now. Walter is in college. Katie is a high school special education teacher. When they return for the holidays, I look for signs of my influence. Are they well-mannered? Do they read? Are they generous? I know that I am a different person having borne and raised them.

I am a different person, too, because I tended to George and Randall. The brothers came to us through the state foster care system. After a year, when the court decided that they couldn't go home, we decided against adoption because two little ones were just too much to absorb into our family. They were adopted by Ellen and John, a childless couple with a welcoming home and love to give them. For five months, we kept in touch to help with the transition, but the only subsequent contact had been a yearly exchange of Christmas cards. I thought we might hear from the boys when, as adults, they became curious about the year of their lives they spent with us. But any signs of my influence would have faded by then.

It is a few days before Christmas. I stand in my kitchen baking cut-out cookies–gingerbread men, Santas, snowmen. Soft flour sifts into the air as I mix it with butter and eggs. The smell of the hot oven and browning cookie edges fills the room. When the telephone rings I wipe my hands on my red apple apron. On the other end of the line is a child who has apparently misdialed a friend's phone number. His words are hurried and garbled. "I'm sorry," I say. "Who are you calling for?"

His words ring clear the second time "This is Randall."

My heart does a little flip, but I am skeptical. "Are you Randall Wall?" I ask.

"Yes," he says.

"Oh, Randall, I am so glad to hear from you. How are you?"

Randall is eleven and in the sixth grade. He likes wood shop best. He remembers us, he claims. When our Christmas card arrived, he had recognized the name and asked his mother if he could call.

"You have a picture of me with long hair," he tells me. "But, my hair isn't that long any more." I have to smile. I have no doubt that he has changed in many ways.

"Is Walter there?" he wants to know. "I remember him,"

"No," I say, "he won't be home from college for a few days."

"What about Katie?"

"She will be home in two days."

"Can you have them call me?"

A few days later, after more telephone calls, we have arranged for Randall and his family visit.

*   *   *

TEN YEARS AGO, when Randall and George came to us, they were two-and-a-half years and nine months old. They were pale, scared, shy babies in diapers who brought with them the baggage of abused children: silence, bruises, a social worker, a guardian ad litem, outgrown clothes packed in a black garbage bag, parents who couldn't cope and the sadness of leaving behind the only world they knew.

During their year with us, they grew into rosy-cheeked, chattering boys who smiled and laughed and hugged. Randall and I had a special bond. He cared whether I smiled or frowned at him. He was jealous of the attention I gave George. He felt free to sneak into the out-of-bounds laundry room one evening and dress in an old shirt of mine. He emerged with a big grin on his face; he knew I wouldn't scold.

Randall learned to speak during his second month with us. One of his first words was "Mommy." He had been with Ellen and John for five months before he was able to sort out who "mommy" was now. One day during the transition period, as I played alone at a park with boys, Randall had turned to me and asked. "So....you aren't my mommy anymore?" Softly, I answered "no" and explained again that Ellen would be his new mommy now. He seemed to absorb the information in a matter-of-fact way. Shortly thereafter, I stopped visiting. But I still felt like his mother.

With his visit pending, I wondered: Can a child have many mothers over the course of a childhood? Can you feel like a mother to a child even though you are long done mothering him? Does being his mother for a year, the year he turns three, the year he learns language, entitle you to the honor of the title "Mother"? Not all mothering is equal, of course, There are layers, classes, ranks, positions. There is the mother who gives birth, stretching her body to give life to a new human being. She plays a special role, no matter how long it lasts. The current mother is always the first violin, a place hard earned, and the rest of us must take second chair. I want to think, though, that all the violins are needed, all their music resonating in the child.

*   *   *

ON THE DAY of the visit, the boys come in the side door that family members always use. "Hi," says Randall. He and George walk quickly past me and rattle off their questions.

"Where's Walter?"

"I remember the front yard, but didn't it use to be much bigger?"

Walter and Katie come down the front stairs and the boys quiet a little–suddenly shy to see my children grown. There are lots of hellos. We greet their parents. I can't take my eyes from Randall. He is as beautiful as ever, with the same black hair, dark red lips, pale skin, rosy cheeks and deep blue eyes.

"I brought that book you gave me," Randall says and holds out the sky-blue vinyl photo album I made for him nine years ago. His name is still written large on the cover in black permanent pen. We put it on the coffee table next to our album from that year.

"First, let's look around," I suggest.

We walk through the house, and I point out the small sunny bedroom they slept in, the backyard patio where they played, the low Japanese maple tree they recognize from a picture in Randall's book. They remember Ginger, our now dead terrier poodle. I tell George that his favorite way to get in trouble was to eat Ginger's food out of her dish. He looks at me as if searching for a flicker of remembering, as if studying my face to see if I am telling the truth.

Later, we sit on the couch in the living room and munch on Christmas cookies and candy. Red and yellow and blue lights on the Christmas tree flash in various patterns. As we turn the pages of my photo album, Randall looks up at me and says: "You look just the same, except your hair is different." Of course, I don't look the same after ten years. But his voice is eager, sincere. Both boys are very generous and open with others, their mother later tells me. A warmth seeps through my chest. My children are like that as well.

We turn to the photos in Randall's book, laid out as I had originally inserted them. The early pictures show him clad only in a diaper and puzzling at the camera. In the later pictures, he is fully dressed, smiling and hugging Katie. At the end of the book are letters we wrote to him before he left: our attempt to explain who we are. (As we did with George, but he didn't bring his book.) Randall wants to read the letter Katie wrote, and Katie nods. She was twelve when she wrote it.

In the few minutes it takes Randall to read the letter out loud, my heart is in my throat and although I follow the words, I find my mind wandering back nine years to the Christmas three months after they left. They came back with Ellen and John for short visit. Randall was still adjusting to the change. He was excited and tripped and hit his head on the coffee table. It took every ounce of self control I could muster not to scoop him up in my arms and soothe away the hurt, but rather to let Ellen, the new mother, the hopefully permanent mother, be the one to step in.

Now, I listen to Randall read Katie's words in a strong voice. "It was fun to have you here with us. It was fun to jump on the beds, play in the sprinkler. We will miss you and love you always." I fight back tears. His look is the open-faced look I remember from his days with us, his willingness to accept what life gives. Was he born with this eagerness, or did we give it to him? Probably both, I decide.

The boys head out to shoot baskets with Katie and Walter, and Ellen and John fill us in on the boys' progress. Randall is active in Boy Scouts. At eleven he has already been on a wilderness adventure and participated in an iron scout competition. George is a good athlete and an excellent, fast skier. When the children return—my four children, I think as they walk in—the boys ask to stay longer. We talk of visiting in the summer when Katie and Walter are again home.

Randall and George initiate hugs, and slowly we make our way outside. At the last minute, I ask Randall for another hug, and he readily wraps his arms around me. I hold him tight. But then I must let him go. As the visitors climb into the car and drive away, I try to hold on to the feeling of his small body against mine. I cry a little for what could have been, and try to hold inside me the memory of what was–the joy I had in tending to him, teaching him to talk, to share, to kick a ball. Those moments still dwell inside me somewhere, though they are fading like old snapshots. Maybe, I think, I can still have "what is." I am one of Randall's mothers. Whether acknowledged or not, each mother is important. Maybe I live a little in Randall's words, his manner, the quickness of his smile, the eagerness of his questions, the strength of his arms as they wrap me in a goodbye embrace.

ABOUT RIDGEWRITERS

Formed in 1976, Ridgewriters is a group of writers in Southeastern Michigan that meets each week to offer each other critiques, advice, and to share ideas and experiences about writing. Gathering in the Spicer House in Farmington Hills, Ridgewriters also participates in various cultural and artistic events in and around the Greater Detroit Area. The membership includes poets, essayists, and novelists of varying levels of experience, from promising amateurs to professional writers.